Bodhicatva

by Fleassy Malay

for Kaia Acacia James
My daughter
My teacher

Written and Illustrated by Fleassy Malay www.fleassymalay.com

CW00956505

Bodhicatva
is a very
contented cat.

He sits all day
by the gate
in the garden

and he smiles.

It's not a false smile,

Or a fake smile.

A hurt smile,

Or a hate smile.

It's that kind
of smile
that comes

from a very deep
happy place

In Spring,
flowers grow up
all around him...

and he smiles.

In Summer,
the sun shines
down hot on
his head...

and he smiles.

In Autumn,
the leaves
turn brown and
fall off the
trees...

and he smiles.

And in Winter...

it snows....

And...

it snows....

And...

But still...

Bodhicatva
is a
VERY

CPSIA information can be obtained at www.ICGtesting.com
Printed in the USA
BVIW12n1442230216
3866BVAU00002B/2

In Buddhist traditions, a Bodhisattva is a being who through deep compassion has reached enlightenment for the benefit of all human beings. It is also said that it is someone who when reaching enlightenment chose not to ascend but to stay in this realm for the sole purpose of teaching the path.

I would like to say a deep thank you to everyone who helped make this book happen.
Kaia for being my inspiration. Jay for being my rock. My parents for their never ending support.
Lindsey for being a true sister. Plus an extra special thank you to every one of you
who funded this project on Pozible, I would not have done it without you.

Contented Cat.